Stegosaur
(7 metres)

Hadrosaur
(10 metres)

Iguanodon
(9 metres)

Diplodocus (30 metres)

Triceratops
Topsy
(14 metres)

Gumdrop
Honorary Dinosaur
(4 metres)

For Mimi,
with my love.

GUMDROP
and the Dinosaur

Written and illustrated by
Val Biro

AWARD PUBLICATIONS LIMITED

Mr Josiah Oldcastle was an old-fashioned man. He wore old-fashioned clothes and drove an old-fashioned car called Gumdrop. He liked it that way. But people teased him about his car: they said it was positively prehistoric, like a dinosaur.

Even his grandson Dan teased him, which annoyed Mr Oldcastle. "Dinosaur, indeed! Gumdrop's a 1926 vintage car and the very best," he said. "But if you want to see a real dinosaur, come out with me tomorrow."

So next day they drove to the Museum. Horace the dog came too, and they walked in.

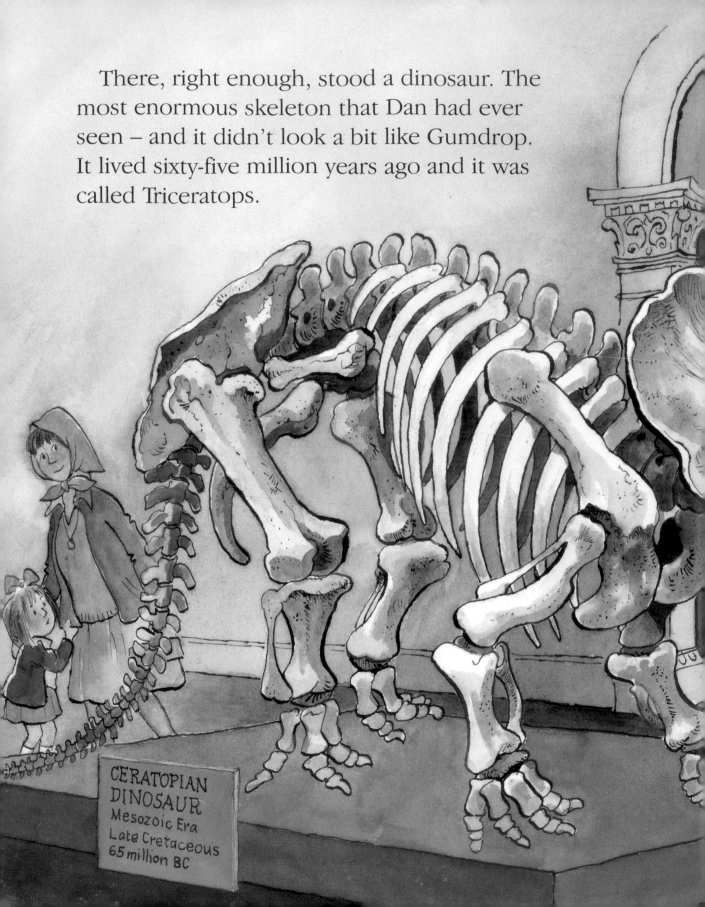

There, right enough, stood a dinosaur. The most enormous skeleton that Dan had ever seen – and it didn't look a bit like Gumdrop. It lived sixty-five million years ago and it was called Triceratops.

CERATOPIAN DINOSAUR
Mesozoic Era
Late Cretaceous
65 million BC

Dan couldn't cope with such a long name, so he decided to call it Topsy for short. Soon he got to like Topsy a lot. Then they left and went to a shop next to the Museum.

TRICERATOPS

It sold computers, and Mr Oldcastle wanted to buy one to show his friends that he wasn't old-fashioned at all. The manager was very helpful.

"There's nothing old-fashioned about these," he said as he produced the latest model, *The Miracle*. It was so new that even he didn't know about everything it could do.

"That's the one for me," said Mr Oldcastle impulsively, and bought it.

He put it on Gumdrop's back seat and wanted to try it out right away, so he fixed the wire to Gumdrop's battery. They climbed into the car and Dan switched the computer on. Nothing happened – until Horace put his big paws on the keyboard and pressed.

Suddenly it seemed as if Gumdrop was racing at an impossible speed, through a whirlwind, backwards.

"Hold tight!" yelled Mr Oldcastle. Then just as suddenly the car stopped. He looked out cautiously – to see a most incredible sight.

Right in front of them stood Topsy the dinosaur, alive and smiling. Behind him stretched a prehistoric landscape, and there was no sign of the Museum or the shop – the whole town had disappeared.

"Hello!" said Topsy. "Welcome back to my own time!"

"This is impossible!" stammered Mr Oldcastle, unable to believe his eyes. "What... what..."

"Grandad!" yelled Dan, "the computer – look!"

The screen showed these words:

TIME:
65 MILLION
YEARS BACK
MESOZOIC ERA
CRETACEOUS PERIOD

So that was it! The computer had turned Gumdrop into a time machine and they were back among the dinosaurs! Then the screen said:

WARNING: Beware of Theropod Dinosaurs!

"Don't worry," said Topsy, "T. Rex and his like are probably extinct by now. But come and meet my friends, Apato, Brachio and Dip."

The huge dinosaurs stared at Gumdrop with apprehension; but when Topsy reassured them, telling them it was only a car, they began to recite a poem.

As you see
    we are gigantic,
But neither bad nor
    mad or frantic;
We eat all day
    and sleep all night
And never get
    into a fight.
For exercise we
    don't take runs,
Because we weigh
    three hundred tons.

Dip (or Diplodocus) picked a flower and
gave it to Dan.

A whole crowd of dinosaurs lumbered into view, each more weird and wonderful than the next. They thought that Gumdrop must be some kind of theropod dinosaur. "He's nothing of the sort," snorted Mr Oldcastle, and got out to teach these creatures about vintage cars.

They listened patiently to the lecture, and didn't understand a word. When it was over at last, they unanimously declared Gumdrop an honorary dinosaur. Mr Oldcastle was rather pleased with this.

"Let's have a race," said Topsy and they all agreed. "Ready, steady, GO!"

Gumdrop shot forward at top speed and all the dinosaurs came thundering after. Even the three poetic ones joined in, because it was so exciting.

"Look at me," yelled Mr Oldcastle, "I'm the fastest dinosaur of the lot!" But he shouldn't have boasted or looked behind him – because the ground suddenly gave way and Gumdrop was axle-deep in a lake.

A Plesiosaur reared up to attack, but Topsy came to the rescue just in time. Then they all heard a frightful sound.

It was the ferocious roar of a huge dinosaur that straddled the ground in front of them.

I am Rex, the carnivore,
The terrible Tyrannosaur!

And Tyrannosaurus Rex
advanced on Gumdrop!

"Oh no you don't," cried Topsy, and charged.
   T. Rex stopped. It was bad enough to be attacked by a Triceratops, but even worse to be attacked by a blue dinosaur on wheels with smoke coming out of its back end.

And when Mr Oldcastle switched on the lights and Gumdrop leaped forward with his horn blaring, T. Rex turned and fled for his life.

He should have looked where he was going, because
he tripped over a boulder, went head over heels, and fell
headlong into a big, black, bottomless pit. The earth
trembled and shook as it swallowed him up. And that
was the end of Tyrannosaurus Rex.

"Phew!" said Mr Oldcastle, "that was a near thing. Anyhow, he's certainly extinct now! Though he might turn up in a museum in sixty-five million years' time!"

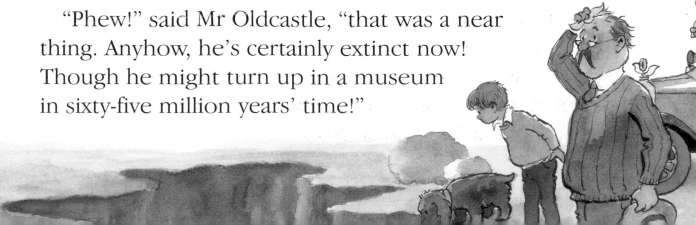

The other dinosaurs
returned when they saw the
end of their enemy. They
danced round Gumdrop in
jubilation.

Topsy prepared a speech
of thanks to Gumdrop, and
everyone sat down to listen.
Including Horace the dog.

But he sat straight on the computer keyboard, and
suddenly Gumdrop seemed to be racing again – but
forwards this time.

"Hold tight!" yelled Mr Oldcastle.

When they stopped, they were in front of the Museum again. Horace must have cancelled the time machine program when he sat on the keyboard, and all went back to normal.

They had enjoyed the adventure, but this computer was too clever for Mr Oldcastle: he took it back and exchanged it for an ordinary one.

He gave it to Dan. "Computers are not for me: I'll just be my old-fashioned self. Mind you, if you ever call Gumdrop a dinosaur again, make sure you call him an *honorary* one!" Then they both had the same thought, and went back to the Museum.

There stood Topsy the dinosaur, sure enough, a skeleton as before. Except that his feet were rather muddy. And Dan was quite certain that the dinosaur had a smile on his face.

ISBN 1-84135-308-6

Copyright © 1988 Val Biro
This edition copyright © 2004 Val Biro

First published 1988 by Hodder and Stoughton Children's Books
This revised edition first published 2004 by Award Publications Limited,
27 Longford Street, London NW1 3DZ

Printed in Malaysia